The Enchanted Book

BY RUTH CHEW

ILLUSTRATED BY THE AUTHOR
COVER ILLUSTRATION BY KAREN BARNES

A
LITTLE APPLE
PAPERBACK

SCHOLASTIC INC.
New York Toronto London Auckland Sydney

ISBN 0-590-09874-8

12 11 10 9 8 7 6 5 4 3 2   9/9 0 1 2 3/0

Printed in the U.S.A.

First Scholastic printing, January 1998

For Edna of the magic ring

1

As soon as he was dressed on Saturday morning, Jay Darby went to his sister's room. She had just finished making her bed.

"Happy birthday, Serena." Jay handed her a flat package wrapped in aluminum foil and tied with a piece of red and white string.

"Thanks, Jay." Serena sat at her desk and started to untie the string.

"I found it in the half-price bookstore," her brother told her. "I went there to look for *King Arthur*. Dad's always telling me to read that. I found a paperback copy of it in the store. Then I saw this. There's no writing in it, but you could draw in it or use it for an address book."

Jay watched Serena take off the foil. Inside was a skinny book covered with cloth embroidered all over with silvery green leaves and lavender flowers.

It was so beautiful that for a moment Serena just stared at it. Then she looked up at her brother with shining eyes. "I love it, Jay. Do you have a pen? I'll write my name in it."

Jay pulled a ballpoint pen out of his shirt pocket and handed it to her. He leaned over to watch while Serena opened the book and touched it with the pen. At once words appeared on the page.

STOP! YOU'LL HURT ME!

"It's magic!" Serena whispered.

Jay stared as the letters faded away. "Modern magic. It must be a new kind of laptop computer."

"But I never typed anything on it," Serena reminded him.

Jay thought about this. "It's voice-programmed to answer certain questions. Ask it something."

Serena was sure the book was magic. She didn't want to risk offending it. "Beautiful Book, what is your name?"

More words appeared on the page.

IF YOU KNEW MY NAME,
YOU MIGHT CALL ME BY IT.
THAT WOULD MEAN BAD LUCK
FOR YOU.

The words stayed on the page long enough for Jay and Serena to read them. Then they faded away.

"It's very cleverly programmed," Jay said. He was a year and a half older than Serena and thought he was too old to believe in magic.

Serena was not going to let him spoil it for her. "I'm sorry I touched you with the pen," she said to the book. "I want to talk to you. Is there something I could call you that is not your name?"

YOU MAY CALL ME
"YOUR MAJESTY."

"Thank you, Your Majesty." Serena shut the book.

Mrs. Darby walked into the room. "I see Jay already gave you his pretty present. There are more gifts for you downstairs. What does the birthday girl want for breakfast?"

While her mother made waffles, Serena unwrapped her presents.

As always, Great Aunt Sally, who lived in Alabama, had sent her a fancy party dress. Serena lived in Brooklyn, where girls her age never wore dresses like that.

"What's in here?" Jay looked at a big package labeled "Happy Birthday to Serena from Mother and Dad."

Jay and Mr. Darby watched Serena open the box. She took out a beautiful pair of Rollerblades.

Serena had longed for in-line skates, but she knew they were expensive. "Oh, thank you, thank you!" Serena hugged her father and ran over to hug her mother too.

Mrs. Darby beamed. "Waffle time!" she said.

The four of them sat down at the breakfast table to eat the waffles while they were hot.

Serena expected Jay to talk about the

book he'd given her, but instead he said, "Those are neat-looking Rollerblades Serena got. Do you think I could have some for my birthday?"

"It's only April. Your birthday's not till November," his mother reminded him.

Mr. Darby laughed. "By that time you may want something quite different."

Jay was very quiet for the rest of the meal. Serena could see that he was thinking hard.

After breakfast Mr. Darby sat down in the living room to read the newspaper. Serena and Jay cleared the table and loaded the dishwasher. Mrs. Darby was busy at the kitchen table cutting circles of waxed paper to line layer cake pans. She looked out of the window. "Oh, dear! It's raining. I was hoping you two would be outdoors for a while."

"We'll try to stay out of your way," Jay said. "Come on upstairs, Serena. Can't you see Mom wants to make your birth-day cake?"

Serena picked up her presents and followed her brother upstairs. He went to her room at the back of the house. "Let's see what His Majesty has to say."

Serena hung the fancy dress in her closet. "I thought I left the book on my desk. It's not here."

She looked on her dresser, in all the drawers of her desk, and in her bookcase, but she couldn't find the book anywhere.

Jay got down on his hands and knees to look under the furniture. The little book wasn't there either. "I don't understand it. If you hadn't seen it too, Serena, I'd think I dreamed the whole thing."

3

"Your Majesty," Serena said. "Where are you?"

The slender book drifted down from the ceiling and landed on Serena's bed.

Serena sat down on one side of it, and Jay sat on the other.

Serena opened the book. "How did you get up there, Your Majesty?"

Words formed on the blank page.

I JUST SPELLED
"HORSE AND HATTOCK."

The book bounced up and down on the bed.

"Horse and Hattock," Jay repeated. "Ow!" His head had bumped into the ceiling.

Serena read aloud from the book.

"YOU MUST BE CAREFUL
WITH SPELLS."

"Ask him how I can get down, Serena," Jay begged.

The book must have heard him. It spelled out.

I AM NOT A HIM!

Serena relayed the message.

"Sorry!" Jay said. "Please, Your Majesty, how do I come down?"

Serena read the answer to him.

"SAY 'HATTOCK AND HORSE'!"

Jay said, "Haddock and Horse!"

Nothing happened.

"What's wrong?" Jay asked. "I said 'Haddock and Horse.'"

"THAT'S WHAT'S WRONG," Serena read.

"A HADDOCK IS A FISH.
HATTOCK IS A SPELL!"

Serena had to read this twice, being very careful to sound her *T*'s.

"Hattock and Horse," Jay said. He floated down to the bed.

"Your Majesty," Serena asked, "why were you up on the ceiling?"

IT HAS BEEN A LONG TIME
SINCE I WAS IN A PLACE WHERE
I COULD LEVITATE. I WANTED TO
PRACTICE. IT CAN BE USEFUL.

"Where were you that you couldn't practice?" Jay wanted to know.

I WAS LOCKED IN DRAWERS
OR CHESTS. PEOPLE WHO SAW WORDS
APPEAR ON MY PAGES THOUGHT
I WAS AN EVIL SPIRIT.
SOME COULDN'T READ.
OTHERS WERE AFRAID TO.

AT LAST I STOPPED SPELLING
ANYTHING ON MY PAGES,
BUT WHEN SERENA TRIED TO WRITE
ON ME, I HAD TO STOP HER.
EVER SINCE I WAS ENCHANTED
MANY YEARS AGO, ONLY YOU TWO
HAVE READ AND ANSWERED ME.

"How did you get in the half-price bookstore?" Jay asked.

A WOMAN FOUND ME IN
A CHEST IN HER ATTIC.
SHE HAD NO USE FOR ME AND
WAS HAPPY TO SELL ME
TO THE BOOKSTORE MAN.

"He told me he put you in a glass case so people could see how beautiful you are," Jay said. "All his customers were looking for storybooks. I wanted a story-book too, but I needed a present for Serena. You looked like something she'd like."

"And I won't lock you in a drawer," Serena promised.

"Only please, Your Majesty," Jay said, "don't let Mom see you levitating."

4

Now that someone was reading what she wrote, Her Majesty kept writing.

WHY DO THOSE BOOTS
HAVE WHEELS, SERENA?

Serena slipped out of her sneakers and put on the Rollerblades. She stood up, but had to hang on to her desk chair to keep from falling.

SO YOU WANT TO TURN
INTO A WAGON!

"You skate on these, and you don't need ice," Jay said, "but there's not enough

room here for Serena to keep her bal-
ance. She ought to be outdoors."

I'VE SEEN PEOPLE WITH
FLAT BONES TIED TO THEIR FEET
SLIDING AROUND ON A FROZEN RIVER
IT SEEMED LIKE FUN.

Serena looked out of the window. "It's
stopped raining, and the sun is shining.
I wish you had Rollerblades too, Jay.
We could go to the park." She sat down
to take off the skates and put on her
sneakers.

Jay pointed to the open book on the
bed.

DO YOU WANT
ROLLERBLADES, JAY?

"Yes, Your Majesty," he said, "but I have
to wait till my birthday in November."

I REMEMBER A SPELL
THAT MAKES ONE THING
EXACTLY LIKE ANOTHER.

15

"That's a clone," Jay said.

I CAN'T WORK SPELLS AS LONG AS
I'M TRAPPED IN THIS SHAPE.
IF YOU TWO DO AS I TELL YOU,
MAYBE WE CAN CAST A SPELL
TOGETHER. SHALL WE TRY?

Serena's heart seemed to skip a beat.
She had always wanted to be mixed up
with magic, but this was scary. "How
about it, Jay?"

Jay grinned. "Count me in! What do we
have to do?"

Her majesty was quick to answer.

WE WILL NEED THE
FOUR ELEMENTS.

The children just stared at each other.
Then Serena went to her desk and looked
in the dictionary. "Earth, air, fire, and
water," she read. "Come on, Jay."

They left the magic book open on the
bed and went downstairs to the kitchen.
Mrs. Darby was busy taking hot pans of

cake out of the oven and setting them on wire racks to cool.

Jay stood on tiptoe to grab a book of safety matches from an upper shelf of the cabinet.

Serena pulled two paper cups from the dispenser and took an old soupspoon out of the catch-all kitchen drawer. She went into the backyard to spoon some dirt into one of the paper cups.

Jay rummaged in the catch-all drawer. He stuffed his pockets with rubber bands of different sizes, an old latex glove, a length of string, a few pencil stubs, a piece of chalk, the lid to a wheat germ jar, and whatever else might be handy to work a magic spell.

Mrs. Darby was trying to find her recipe for "Miracle Frosting." She didn't even look up when Serena came in from the garden and went back upstairs with Jay.

5

The magic book was right where they'd left it on the bed. As soon as Jay and Serena came near, letters appeared on the page.

DO YOU HAVE THE ELEMENTS?

"I don't want to make Fire till we're ready, Your Majesty," Jay said.

"Here's Earth." Serena put the paper cup of dirt on her desk. "I'll get Water from the bathroom later. If I left it around in a paper cup, it might spill. How long does it take to work the spell?"

NO TIME AT ALL IF IT'S DONE RIGHT.
YOU'VE FORGOTTEN AIR!

Jay pulled the latex glove from his pocket and blew into it until it was filled with Air. He held it tight and closed the cuff with a rubber band. "How's this?"

VERY STRANGE, BUT IT
OUGHT TO WORK. DO YOU HAVE
A LOOKING GLASS?

"There's one on the door." Serena closed the door of her room and held the magic book in front of the mirror on it.

She saw words appear on the book in the mirror, but they were backward. She turned the book around and read:

TOO BIG. THE MIRROR
HAS TO GO IN THE
MIDDLE OF THE FLOOR
NEXT TO THE ROLLERBLADES.

Serena put the magic book on her bed again. She went to get a mirror from her mother's dresser. "Can you see the floor from where you are, Your Majesty?"

WHEN THE BOOK IS OPEN,
I CAN SEE ANYTHING IN THE ROOM.

The book told them what to do. Jay rolled up the rag rug. He took the chalk from the pocket of his jeans, tied it to one end of the string, and handed the other end to Serena. "Hold this tight to the floor."

Using the string as a compass, Jay drew a circle with the chalk. He put the Rollerblades in the center of the circle.

The mirror had a folding stand. It was in a round frame with mirrors on both front and back. Serena stood it carefully in the circle where it would reflect the Rollerblades.

She went to get Water in the empty paper cup and set it on the chalk circle across from the cup of Earth. The Air-filled glove rested on the circle between the paper cups.

Jay put the lid from the wheat germ jar on the circle across from the glove. "I took wood shavings from the pencil sharpener to use as fuel," he said. "And I'm going to build a little Fire in this lid."

Suddenly Serena remembered. "We're not allowed to play with fire!"

"It's quite safe." Jay took the matchbook from his pocket, opened it, and pulled off a match. He carefully closed the matchbook. "Look!"

He struck the match, and it burst into flame.

Her Majesty rose off the bed and floated in front of their faces.

BLOW THAT OUT! DO YOU WANT
TO SET THE HOUSE ON FIRE?

6

For a moment they were both too startled to move. Then Serena blew out the match.

"But, Your Majesty," Jay argued, "we need Fire to work the spell."

YOU HAVE ALL THE MAGIC OF FIRE
IN THAT LITTLE SQUARE THING
IN YOUR HAND.
PUT THAT ON THE CIRCLE.

Jay picked up the jar lid and put the match folder in its place. "Now what, Your Majesty?"

I JUST NOTICED THAT
YOUR FEET ARE BIGGER
THAN SERENA'S.
THE ROLLERBLADE BOOTS WILL BE
TOO SMALL FOR YOU.

THEY'LL BE JUST LIKE SERENA'S.
THERE'S NO USE WORKING THE SPELL.

Jay was angry, but all he said was: "You mean we went to all this trouble for nothing?"

I'M SORRY.
I WAS ONLY TRYING TO HELP.

"Please, Your Majesty," Serena begged, "let's go ahead with the spell anyway, just to see if it really will work."

OF COURSE IT WILL WORK!
IF YOU DON'T BELIEVE ME, JUST
WALK THREE TIMES AROUND
THE CIRCLE WHILE YOU KEEP
CHANTING THE WORDS ROF BAM.

It wasn't easy to walk around the circle. It was so close to the bed on one side that Serena and Jay had to step up onto the bed and then down again as they went around the circle chanting "Rof Bam! Rof Bam! Rof Bam!" over and over.

They were both out of breath and had

lost count of how many times they'd marched around the circle when the magic book flew in front of them to signal: STOP! MY MAGIC STILL WORKS!

Jay was edging past Serena's desk. She was marching over the bed. They looked at the center of the circle.

Now there were two pairs of Roller-blades there.

Serena whispered to her brother, "Look!"

Jay saw that one pair was bigger than the other.

"They might fit me." Jay took off his sneakers and shoved his feet into the boots of the Rollerblades. They were a bit loose. Jay went to get his wool socks. With the socks, the fit was almost perfect.

The magic book stated:

THIS HAS NEVER HAPPENED
BEFORE. WHAT WAS DIFFERENT
ABOUT THIS SPELL?

"The mirror, Your Majesty." Serena hopped off the bed and picked up the mirror. She turned it so that first one side and then the other faced the magic book.

"The glass is flat on one side," Serena told her. "The other side is curved to make things look bigger. I had the curved side reflecting the Rollerblades. I didn't know if it would work in the spell. And I didn't want Jay to laugh at me if it didn't."

I WAS AFRAID I'D FORGOTTEN
HOW TO WORK A SPELL.
THANK YOU, SERENA.
YOU TAUGHT ME A NEW TRICK.

7

"Lunchtime!" Mrs. Darby was calling from downstairs.

Jay took off the Rollerblades and heavy socks and put on his sneakers. He pushed the skates under the bed. "I don't know what Mom would think if she saw them."

Serena took the mirror back to her mother's dresser. She dumped out the water, folded the damp paper cup, and tucked it into the pocket of her jeans. Then she put the cup of dirt, the match folder, and the air-filled glove in the bottom drawer of her desk. "Just in case we want to cast another spell."

The magic book was still open on the bed. Serena laid it on top of her desk. She was about to close it when words flashed on the page.

THE SPELL LASTS
ONLY FOUR HOURS!

"Look, Jay," Serena said.

Her brother read the message. He was trying to rub out the chalk circle by scuffing it with his sneakers, but he couldn't even smear it. Jay unrolled the rag rug to cover the circle.

Mrs. Darby was calling again. Jay and Serena had to go downstairs for lunch.

Mr. Darby was already seated at the dining room table. "It's turned out to be a nice day," he said. "There'll be a ball game on television after all."

When they'd finished their soup and sandwiches, Mrs. Darby said, "Who wants to lick the frosting bowl?" She was surprised that Serena and Jay didn't start to fight over it, but neither one said anything.

The spell would last only four hours. They were in a hurry to go outdoors with the Rollerblades.

Mr. Darby grinned. "If nobody else wants to lick that bowl, I sure do." He went into the kitchen.

Serena and Jay cleared the table and loaded the dishwasher.

Jay put in the last bowl. "Serena wants to try out her Rollerblades, Mom. The sidewalks around here are all uneven. We'd like to go to the park."

"Good idea," his mother said. "Traffic is banned in the park on weekends. She could practice on the roadway."

Mrs. Darby handed Serena a strong plastic bag from a shoe store to carry the Rollerblades and hold her sneakers when she took them off.

"I could us a bag like that too," Jay said.

Mrs. Darby found one for him in her collection of bags.

Jay and Serena went upstairs to get the Rollerblades. The magic book was still open on the desk. As soon as they came into the room, words started to appear on the page.

YOU'VE BEEN GONE A LONG TIME.
I WAS LONELY.

8

"I'm sorry, Your Majesty. We had to help Mom clean up after lunch." Serena said.

She put her Rollerblades into the plastic bag. Jay pulled his from under her bed. He tugged at his sister's arm to show her that words were appearing again on the page of the magic book.

WHAT ARE YOU GOING
TO DO NOW?

"We're going to the park," Jay told her.

TAKE ME WITH YOU!
I HAVEN'T SEEN A TREE
OR THE SKY FOR YEARS.

"How can we take you, Your Majesty?" Serena asked.

LEAVE ME OPEN AND
PUT ME IN YOUR POCKET.

"Even closed, you won't fit in my pocket," Serena argued. "And Jay's are always full of junk."

I CAN BE ANY SIZE I LIKE.
I JUST CAN'T CHANGE THE SHAPE
I'VE BEEN TURNED INTO.

The magic book began to shrink. Before Serena and Jay knew what was happening, it was small enough to fit into any pocket. It rose up off the desk and dived down into Jay's shirt pocket.

For almost a minute neither of the

children could say a word. Then Jay spoke. "You win, Your Majesty. We'll take you to the park." He packed his Rollerblades and thick socks in the bag Mrs. Darby had given him.

When they went to get their jackets from the hall closet downstairs, Jay put the tiny book in his jacket pocket.

Prospect Park was several blocks away from their house. It is so large that there are lakes and meadows and woods there.

As soon as they were outdoors, the book sailed up out of Jay's pocket and flew at eye level between the two children. With its cover open, it looked like a pretty butterfly.

At Church Avenue, cars and trucks went rattling and screeching by. When a bus rumbled along, sending out clouds of smoke, the tiny book dived back into Jay's pocket. He could feel it trembling.

Jay stroked it gently with one finger. "Don't be afraid."

The book slipped out of his pocket and flew between Serena and Jay. It became just big enough for them to read the words: IT'S A DRAGON!

"No, it isn't," Serena told her. "It's just a big wagon. There aren't any wagons like that in the park."

LET ME KNOW WHEN
WE COME TO THE PARK.

The book shrank until it could dive back into Jay's pocket and be out of sight.

9

Spring had arrived in Prospect Park. The willows by the lake were green. Three twisted trees nearby sprouted little pink buds. A robin was trying to pull a worm out of the muddy edge of the bridle path. From the top of a tall tree a mockingbird began to sing.

The tiny book slipped out of Jay's pocket and floated in front of the children's faces. It became big enough for them to read:

I WANT TO LOOK AROUND.
I'LL BE BACK LATER.
DON'T LEAVE WITHOUT ME.

Her Majesty waited until Serena and Jay had read her message. Then the book shrank until it was even smaller than before. It floated away across the park.

34

There were no cars on the winding road. It was crowded with people jogging, riding bicycles, pushing baby carriages, and Rollerblading.

Serena followed Jay to the nearest empty bench. She took off her sneakers and put on her brand-new Rollerblades.

Jay took longer to change. He had to get into the thick socks and then into the Rollerblades they'd made with Her Majesty's magic.

The children put their sneakers into the plastic bags and made their way to the road.

The Rollerblades were harder to manage than their old skates. Jay's friend Rick had Rollerblades. He sometimes let Jay try them, so Jay knew enough to give Serena a few tips. In a little while she could skate almost as well as he did.

"It feels like flying," Serena said. She skated on, past the lake and around the tree-covered hill called Lookout Mountain. Jay was right behind her.

At first they were the only people on the road here. Then two teenage boys came down out of the woods.

"Wait a minute!" the taller one called. "I want to ask you something."

Serena coasted to a stop. The boy ran over and put his hand on her arm.

Jay skated over to his sister. The other boy walked over to him.

Serena looked at the two big boys. "What do you want to know?"

The tall boy smiled in a nasty way. "Where did you find those Rollerblades, girlie? They look like the ones I left on a bench near the lake. You'd better give them to me."

"They're a birthday present from my mother and father," Serena told him. "And they're too small to fit you."

"She's right," the other boy said. "But look at these." He pointed to the Rollerblades Jay was wearing.

"Here, you hold on to the girl while I take his skates." The tall boy let go of Serena's arm and rushed to tackle Jay.

10

Jay sat down on the road and started to take off his Rollerblades. "Are you sure you want these skates? They're not the real thing, and they won't last long."

"Shut up and hand them over," the big boy snarled.

Jay had one skate off. He gave it to the boy. He took his sneakers out of the bag and put one on.

While the boy took off his shoe and stuck his foot into the skate boot, Jay slid out of the other Rollerblade. He stuffed the thick socks into his plastic bag and put on his sneakers. "How does that fit you?" he asked.

"A lot better than I thought it would," the boy said. "Hey, Shorty, maybe the girl's skates would fit you."

The shorter boy was holding on to Serena. He looked down at her skates. "Take those off, girlie. I want to try them."

Jay rushed over to him. "Leave my sister alone!"

Shorty was much bigger and stronger than Jay. He let go of Serena and raised his fist to strike her brother.

Serena skated right into Shorty. The two fell to the ground.

Serena tried to stand, but her feet in the skates rolled out from under her.

Jay grabbed her hand to pull her up.

Shorty was on his feet now, and the other boy was skating over to them.

"Horse and Hattock!" Serena yelled.

"Horse and Hattock!" Jay whispered, being careful to sound his *t*'s.

The two children rose up into the air.
"Look!" Jay pointed at the road below.
Serena looked down.

The big boy was staring at his feet. The
Rollerblades had vanished.

Jay grinned. "I thought the four hours
were just about up," he said.

11

"It's scary to say the magic words for up or down," Serena said.

Jay nodded. "We don't know how far up or down they might take us."

Serena tried kicking with her feet and pushing back the air with her hands. She hung the plastic bag over one arm to make this easier. "Look, Jay. It's like swimming!"

Jay pushed his arm through the loops on his bag and put his hands together to point toward the top of Lookout Mountain. He kicked his feet and sailed up over the big hill. Serena followed close behind him.

Their feet were just a little higher than the treetops. In front of them a little fleck of paper was bobbing in the air. It became bigger and bigger.

Serena started to tread air to stay in one place. "Stop, Jay! It's Her Majesty."

The magic book was open. It hovered in front of them.

I SEE THAT THE ENCHANTED
SKATES VANISHED. I HOPE
IT DIDN'T HAPPEN AT A BAD TIME.

Jay laughed. "It couldn't have been better."

LEAD ME BACK TO YOUR
HOUSE. I WANT TO BE SURE
I KNOW THE WAY.

"We'd better not be seen around home like this," Jay said. "Prepare for a landing, Serena. Hattock and Horse!"

"Hattock and Horse," Serena echoed him.

The two children dropped down through the trees. They landed on the walkway that went up and over Lookout Mountain. The magic book floated between them.

Serena sat down on the walk to take off her skates and put on her sneakers. She caught sight of a four-leaf clover poking out of the ground. It seemed a shame to pick it and have it die. Serena dug up the little plant and put it, along with some dirt, into the paper cup in her pocket. Then she stood up and looked around.

At this time there was no one here but Serena, Jay, and Her Majesty.

HAVE YOU EVER BEEN
ON THIS HILL AT NIGHT?

"Oh, no, Your Majesty. It's not safe to be here after dark."

I'M GLAD YOU KNOW THAT.
IT COULD BE DANGEROUS FOR YOU.

Walking on the ground felt strange after swimming through the air.

The magic book became very small and floated just above Serena and Jay. They went down the wide steps of the walkway.

At the foot of the hill they made their way over to the low stone wall that went around the lake.

At one place a man was feeding a crowd of quacking ducks. Farther along, a lady and two little girls were tossing bread to a pair of beautiful white swans. Close to a willow tree, a gray-haired man with a pail pulled his fishing line out of the water.

Serena and Jay turned away from the lake and crossed the highway. Most of the people who had been riding bicycles, skating, and jogging had left.

The children walked to the park gate. The tiny book came after them.

All the way home Her Majesty kept just behind them. At their front door, she dived into Jay's jacket pocket.

Serena rang the doorbell.

Mrs. Darby opened the door and gave each of her children a hug. "You were gone so long I was beginning to worry. It's almost suppertime. Hurry and get washed."

Jay and Serena raced upstairs. Her Majesty slipped out of Jay's pocket and flew down the hall. When Serena reached her room at the back of the house, the magic book had returned to its usual size and was lying open on Serena's desk.

She left it there and went to wash her hands and go down to supper.

12

Supper was a family birthday party.

Mr. Darby had blown up balloons and hung them from the chandelier.

Mrs. Darby had cooked Serena's favorite dinner, roast chicken with stuffing. The birthday cake was covered with wonderful chocolate Miracle Frosting and had "Happy Birthday Serena" written on it in pink icing.

Serena was not good at blowing out candles, but she had decided on a very

special wish. When the candles were lit, she took a deep breath and blew as hard and long as she could. Finally, the last candle flickered out.

"You did it, Serena!" Her mother started to cut the cake.

When supper was over and the kitchen was clean, Mrs. Darby joined her husband to watch the news on television.

Serena and Jay went up to Serena's room. As soon as they walked in the door, words appeared on the magic book.

OPEN THE WINDOW.
I WANT TO GO AND SEE IF
I'M RIGHT ABOUT THAT HILL.

"I thought you said it was dangerous at night, Your Majesty," Jay said.

DANGEROUS FOR YOU TWO.
NOT FOR ME.

NOW OPEN THE WINDOW, AND LEAVE
IT OPEN SO I WON'T HAVE TO BANG
MYSELF OUT OF SHAPE TO GET BACK IN.

The book began to shrink. Serena
opened the window a crack. When Her
Majesty was small enough, she slipped
out and flew away toward the park.

"I wanted to work some more magic,"
Serena said. "Now what do we do?"

"I'm going to read *King Arthur*," Jay
told her.

"You're lucky. I've read every book I
have," Serena said. "Jay, do you think we
could clone your book?"

"We could try," Jay said.

Serena looked in her desk drawer. "We
still have the four Elements, all but
Water. We need a fresh paper cup." She
went down to the kitchen to get one.

Jay rolled up the rag rug. The chalk
circle was as good as new. He went to
get Mrs. Darby's mirror and the book of

King Arthur and put them in the center of the circle. He opened the book so it could stand in front of the mirror.

The cover showed a knight on horseback riding past a castle under a clear blue sky. A wide moat went around the castle, and the drawbridge was up. Both horse and rider wore armor, and both their faces were hidden by their helmets.

When Serena came back with Water,

she helped her brother set the four Elements on the circle. Then they started chanting "Rof Bam! Rof Bam! over and over, walking around the circle, up onto the bed and down, around and around.

They lost count of how many times they went around. They were both too dizzy to notice that the bed had become a hump and the floor was uneven. Suddenly they heard the loud whinny of a horse.

13

At the sound of the horse's neigh, both Jay and Serena blinked their eyes.

Right in front of them they saw a pair of enormous hooves. They looked up.

A huge horse towered over them. The rider was yanking at the reins to stop the horse from trampling the two children.

"Get out of the way!" a hollow voice yelled.

Jay grabbed his sister's hand and pulled her out of the path of the horse and rider. "I'm sorry," he said. "I didn't see you coming."

"I didn't see you, either," the hollow voice said.

Now both Serena and Jay saw that the rider wore a spooky-looking metal helmet that covered his face and had only a narrow slit for him to see through.

"Can you see us now, with that thing on your head?" Serena asked.

"Not well. I'll take it off." The man on the horse tried to pull off his gloves. This was difficult because the back of each glove, fingers and all, was covered with metal plates.

Jay and Serena went over to reach up and help him to free his hands. Then he lifted the helmet off his head and smiled at them.

He climbed down from the horse and held out his hand to each of them in turn. "I'm glad to meet you." His voice wasn't hollow now.

He had sandy brown hair and freckles and didn't look more than seventeen. He seemed strong and healthy, but he wasn't as tall as their father. "What's your name?" he asked. "I'm Sir Miles Dubose, and I'm a knight-errant."

Serena shook his hand. "I'm Serena Darby, and this is my brother, Jay."

"I'm glad to meet you, Sir Miles." Jay clasped his hand. "I've heard about knights, but we don't have them in our country. I thought they were older than you. I don't think my sister knows just what a knight-errant is."

Jay didn't know either, but he wouldn't admit it.

Sir Miles was happy to tell him. "A knight-errant is one who travels in search of adventures to prove his bravery and generosity. He helps people in need."

The young knight began to take off the rest of his armor and pack it into saddle-bags on the horse. "I'm glad to get out of that gear. It's hot and heavy."

"Why were you wearing it?" Serena asked.

"I was going to a tournament," Sir

Miles told her, "but when I came to this evil castle I knew I had gone astray. Why are you here?"

"We don't know why," Jay said. "We don't even know where we are."

"I can't leave you in this dread place." Sir Miles lifted the scary helmet from his horse's head. Jay and Serena helped unstrap the plates of armor from the horse's chest and back.

When the armor was packed away, Sir Miles led the horse by the reins, and Serena and Jay walked beside him, leaving the castle behind.

14

Sir Miles walked as fast as he could. Serena and Jay had to run to keep up with him. Several times the knight turned to look back at the castle. Then he walked even faster. The way led across a sunny meadow. By the time they came to the dark forest on the other side, they were all out of breath.

The path here was too narrow for Serena and Jay to walk beside the knight. For a while they followed the horse.

When they stepped out of the shadows into a sunny glade, the big horse spotted a patch of clover and refused to walk any farther.

"You're hungry, Rocky." Sir Miles patted the horse's neck. "And you must be tired. I know I am." He sat down on a fallen log. "Come and rest," he said to the children. "Now you can tell me your story."

Jay and Serena sat on the mossy ground facing him. While Rocky munched away, they took turns telling Sir Miles all about the magic book and how they were trying to work the spell they'd done before with Her Majesty's help.

"Only it didn't work," Serena said, "and we ended up in front of Rocky's hooves."

Jay nodded. "We must have done something wrong."

"Magic is dangerous," Sir Miles whispered. "In our country there's a lot of it going on."

"I always thought it would be fun," Serena told him. "And I'm sure Her Majesty liked to work magic, but she hated somebody else working it and turning her into a book."

Jay was thinking hard. "If there are people here who understand magic, maybe they could tell us how to break the spell that was cast on Her Majesty."

"There are three powerful workers of magic here," Sir Miles said in a low voice. "Morgan le Fay is a wicked enchantress. Merlin, the King's adviser, is a magician. And Nimue, called the Lady of the Lake, is a good fairy. I've never met any one of them. I don't know where to find Merlin or Nimue, and I don't want anything to do with Morgan le Fay. Still, it's my knightly duty to help you." Sir Miles stood up and walked over to his horse.

Just then a sweet-faced girl with long blond braids stepped into the little glade. She looked about sixteen years old and was prettier than anybody Serena had ever seen, even on television.

The girl was wearing a long blue dress and carrying a basket of little reddish brown apples.

Sir Miles bowed to her. She held up an apple and curtsied. "Will you honor me by accepting this little gift?" He bowed again and took the apple. The girl turned and handed an apple to Serena and one to Jay.

The knight and the children thanked her. Sir Miles couldn't stop looking at her lovely face.

"I must be dreaming," Serena said to herself. "She's too beautiful to be true."

15

"These are very special apples," the girl said. "I've never tasted any like them. Do me the honor of letting me know what you think of them."

Serena bit into the apple. It was crisp and cool, and she was thirsty. She waited to hear what Jay and Sir Miles would say. She watched her brother chomp into the apple.

Now she was sure she was dreaming. Jay was getting smaller every second. In almost no time he was covered with fur and looked like a little dog standing on his hind legs. He got down on all fours, wagged his tail, and ran over to the beautiful girl. She patted him on the head.

Serena looked around for Sir Miles. She couldn't see him anywhere. In his place stood a sandy brown donkey. The girl climbed onto the donkey's back.

The little dog ran over to Serena and stood on his hind legs to look up into her face. She put her fingers under his chin and gazed into his eyes. Suddenly he looked like Jay again. The little dog had vanished.

Now Serena knew that this was not a dream. It was black magic, but for some reason it had no power over her.

She ran over to the donkey and threw her arms around him. At once she found she was hugging Sir Miles.

He was standing up. The beautiful girl was clinging to his back. She slipped off and ended sitting on the ground.

"Let me help you. Your dress will get dirty." Serena grabbed the girl's hand to pull her to her feet.

As soon as Serena touched her, the beautiful girl let out a groan and started to slowly fade from sight. As she faded she became plainer and sadder than any girl Serena had ever known.

At the same time she seemed to dissolve under Serena's fingers. In a little while the girl had melted into the air.

All that was left was the basket of apples.

Sir Miles dug a hole with his sword. Jay buried the basket and went to pat the horse. Rocky didn't seem to mind that he was still loaded down with two big saddle-bags.

"They really were delicious apples." Sir Miles sighed. "And she was such a very pretty girl!"

"I liked being a dog," Jay said. "Why did you have to go and spoil everything, Serena?"

"I couldn't help it," Serena told him. "Maybe I'm allergic to magic. No, that can't be right. Magic must be allergic to me. But I'm sure I was supposed to turn into something. I wonder what it was."

By now Rocky had eaten all the clover. Sir Miles picked up the reins and led the way back into the forest.

16

Sir Miles said he had to go first on the narrow path because he knew the way. Jay wanted to hold the reins and lead the horse. Serena walked after the knight, and Jay followed with Rocky.

Sir Miles looked sad. For a long time he was quiet. Then Serena heard him mutter, "I'm such a fool!"

She moved alongside him. "What's the matter, Sir Miles?"

"Everything," he said. "I guess I'm not meant to be a knight-errant. First I lose my way and miss the tournament. Then I get a chance to rescue you and your brother, and instead you rescue me!"

"Neither of those things is your fault," Serena told him.

"Oh, yes, they are," he insisted. "I hate tournaments. You have to fight people just to prove you're a better knight, not because they've done anything wrong. And you have to kill a knight if he won't surrender. I didn't lose my way on purpose, but I wasn't sorry to miss the tournament."

"But you did the right thing," Serena said. "Think how you'd feel if you killed somebody. And how could it be your fault about the pretty girl?"

"Remember the castle where we met?" Sir Miles asked. "I'd been warned that it belongs to Morgan le Fay, the enchantress. She sends beautiful maidens from there to trap careless passersby. I hurried away from the castle, and I thought we were safe. I should have warned you to beware of those apples. But I forgot everything when I saw that lovely face. If not for you I'd be a donkey now, working in that castle."

"But you're not a donkey," Serena said. "And you are helping us."

Jay was walking right behind his sister and the knight. He heard every word. "Serena's right, Sir Miles," he said. "And I hope you and I learned something."

Sir Miles laughed. "You mean, be careful not to eat apples from beautiful girls!" He changed the subject and lowered his voice. "Do you see that hill?" He pointed to a tree-covered hill in the forest ahead.

"It's getting on toward evening. We'd better not come too close to it."

Serena looked at the hill. "What does it remind you of, Jay?"

Jay squinted his eyes to see better. "I don't know what it is about it, but somehow it reminds me of Lookout Mountain in Prospect Park."

"It looks to me like a hollow hill," Sir Miles told them. "They're safe enough in the daytime, but I don't want to be near one after dark." He started to walk faster.

They left the path where it went close to the hill and circled around, stumbling through underbrush to get back to the path farther on.

17

"What's so scary about a hollow hill?" Serena asked Sir Miles.

"The fairy folk build their palaces inside hollow hills. You can only see them from a distance. Some people see lights burning there with no fuel to keep them going."

"We have lights you don't need fire for," Jay said.

"But they do have fuel," Serena reminded her brother. "It's electricity, the thing that makes lightning flash," she told the knight. "Tell us about the fairy folk, Sir Miles. Are they tiny people?"

"They can be any size they want to be,

or they can be invisible. Often you can't tell them from humans. They never swear to the truth, because they are always truthful. They are loving and generous and reward kindness, but they deeply resent any injury done to them. They know how to levitate and ride through the air and levitate others."

"They don't sound bad," Jay said. "Why are you so afraid of them?"

"Everybody with any sense is," Sir Miles answered. "Maybe it's people like Morgan le Fey who cause that. She's half fairy and half human. Besides, it's dangerous to wander into the invisible palaces of the fairy folk. A few moments there might be a hundred years of our time." He began to walk faster. "If we stop talking, we may be able to get out of the forest before dark. I know a hermit who might let us spend the night in his cave."

A cave sounded so interesting that Jay

and Serena stopped talking and began to walk as fast as they could.

They came out of the forest and were about to cross a little bridge over a winding stream.

The horse reared up on his hind legs and whinnied.

"What's the matter, Rocky?" Sir Miles asked.

"I think I see somebody under the bridge," Jay told him.

The knight pulled a long, shining sword out of the scabbard that hung from his belt. "Come out into the open, whoever you are," he said.

A man in a long brown gown stepped from the shadows under the bridge onto the green bank on the other side of the stream. He shaded his eyes against the glare of the setting sun. "You sound like my old friend Miles."

"Brother Donald, I didn't expect you here!" Sir Miles exclaimed. "I was just on the way to your cave. I hoped you could give my young friends and me shelter for the night."

"I'd be happy to," the hermit told him. "But someone else wanted to move in there, and I thought it wise to move out. We could all sleep under the bridge here. I have a fire and the makings of a stew. We can be quite cozy."

18

Sir Miles led Rocky across the bridge and down the green bank there. Serena and Jay followed.

Brother Donald had laid dry rushes on the damp ground under the end of the bridge. He had taken stones from the river to make a place to build his fire. A black iron pot was bubbling away.

The hermit tossed chunks of meat and vegetables into the pot. "The people who passed this way today were generous with their food and even gave me this pot to cook it in," he explained. "I warned them not to go near my cave. I must warn you too. I left in such a hurry this morning that I didn't have time to put up a DANGER! sign."

Sir Miles begged Brother Donald to tell him who had moved into his cave, but the hermit would only say, "I escaped with my life. You might not be so lucky."

Sir Miles took the harness and the saddlebags off the horse, and Rocky found a patch of grass to nibble.

It was dark by the time the stew was ready. There were no forks or plates. Sir Miles speared chunks of food with his hunting knife to get them out of the pot. They all ate with their fingers.

Serena and Jay enjoyed the meal more than any they could remember.

No dishes had to be washed. Nobody took a bath. They didn't even take off their shoes. Everybody curled up near the fire and fell fast asleep.

When Serena opened her eyes, it was broad daylight. She sat up and looked around.

Brother Donald was boiling oats in the iron pot. Sir Miles and Jay were still sleeping.

Serena stood up and stretched. She washed her face in the cool stream. Then she went to talk to the hermit.

Brother Donald handed her a stick to stir the porridge. "I left all my things behind in the cave," he told her.

"Why won't you tell us who moved into it?" Serena asked.

The hermit put a finger to his lips. "Sir

Miles is so excited about being a knight-errant. He thinks he has to be doing brave deeds and rescuing people. He would be certain to get himself killed. I don't want that. He's a nice lad."

When the porridge was cooked, Brother Donald took the pot off the fire. By the time Jay and Sir Miles woke up, the porridge was cool enough for them to scoop it up in their hands and eat out of them. This was messy, but they couldn't think of any other way to do it.

Afterward they all washed their faces in the stream. It was the second time for Serena. Jay decided to wash his ears as well.

19

Sir Miles wanted to wear his armor. Jay took it out of the saddlebags. While the knight put on his armor, Jay strapped Rocky into the horse's helmet and breast-plate.

Before they said good-bye, the knight thanked the hermit for his hospitality.

"It was good of you to share your food with us," Serena said.

"Especially when you didn't have much," Jay told him.

Brother Donald smiled. "I don't often get a chance to do that. It has made me very happy."

Sir Miles led Rocky up the green bank to a lane beside the stream. Jay helped him mount the horse. The lane was just wide enough for Jay and Serena to walk one on each side of the knight.

On the other side of the lane, rough

grass and prickly gorse bushes grew at the base of a steep, tree-covered cliff.

Sir Miles kept looking up at the cliff. "Brother Donald's cave is up there," he said. "I can spot it by the smoke from his cooking fire. I don't usually wear my helmet. I can't see very well with it on. Let me know if you see signs of a fire."

"Brother Donald didn't want you to go to his cave," Serena reminded the knight.

"He's a holy man and wants peace at any price, but I have sworn to defend the weak." Sir Miles told her. "It's my duty to chase the invader out of that cave and return it to its rightful owner."

Jay was watching the cliff. "What's that up there?"

Serena looked where he was pointing, high up on the cliff. She saw puffs of yellow smoke and what seemed like leaping flames. Whoever was up there must have a roaring bonfire. Serena put her finger to her lips to stop Jay from talking about it. She didn't want Sir Miles to get into a fight and be killed.

But the knight had heard Jay. He looked up at the fire. "You two stay here," he commanded. Then he galloped across the rough ground to a path that led up the hill. Rocky seemed to know the way.

"You never should have showed him the fire, Jay," Serena said. "What'll we do now?"

"Horse and Hattock!" her brother cried, and started to rise in the air.

"Horse and Hattock!" Serena followed him. They used their arms and legs to swim through the air after Rocky and Sir Miles. Soon they hovered close behind the horse and rider.

As he came near the top of the cliff, Sir Miles went more slowly. Ahead of him was a smelly cloud of yellow smoke and darting orange flames.

Serena and Jay looked hard into the smoke and flames. They saw the opening of a cave. Curled in the doorway was a huge, spiny creature, with a head, jaws, and powerful claws like a crocodile. But it was not a crocodile! It had a long snake-like body, batlike wings, and a tail with a wicked-looking stinger on the end.

The stinking fumes came from the yellow smoke pouring out of the creature's nostrils, and the flames blazed from the fiery tongue in its mouth.

It was a dragon!

Sir Miles aimed his lance at the strange creature and put his spurs to the horse.

Rocky charged forward into the smoke and flames.

The dragon's hide was as strong as steel. The wooden shaft of the lance broke in half. Sir Miles jumped down from his horse and pulled his sword from its scabbard. He stepped forward to sink the sword into the dragon, but the smoke blinded him.

The dragon slid over to the knight and opened its terrible jaws wide.

20

Jay swam right into the cloud of smoke. He yanked something from the crowded pocket of his jeans and pitched it into the open mouth of the dragon.

The fire died out. When the smoke cleared, there was no sign of the dragon. In its place was a little gray donkey.

Sir Miles was still blinking from the smoke.

"Hattock and Horse!" Jay drifted down to land beside the donkey.

"Hattock and Horse!" Serena came down next to him. She reached out to pet the donkey.

Her brother dragged her away. "Don't you dare touch him!" Jay hissed. "He'll turn back into a dragon."

Now Serena knew what had happened. "Where'd you get the apple?"

"I saved one and put it into a saddle-bag, just in case it might come in handy. I took it out when I dug out the armor this morning."

Jay walked over to the knight. "You sure gave that dragon a scare! He just disappeared when you pulled out that big sword. And it seems as if he won't come back."

Sir Miles was still blinking the smoke out of his eyes when they heard a rustling sound. Someone was coming up the path to the cave. The knight raised his sword. "Who goes there?"

"Your friend, Brother Donald. Calm down and don't kill me. What's been going on here?" The hermit waited until Sir Miles put away his sword. Then he came over to the cave. "What did you do with my fiery friend?"

"I seem to have scared him away," Sir Miles said.

"I hope you didn't hurt him," the hermit continued. "After all, it isn't his fault he's a dragon."

The little gray donkey trotted over to lick Brother Donald's hand. The hermit stroked the donkey's nose.

"Why are you here now, Brother Donald?" Sir Miles asked. "And why didn't you tell me it was a dragon who had taken over your cave?"

"Would it have stopped you from wanting to drive out the invader?" Brother Donald asked.

"Of course not," the knight replied. "It would only have made me more eager to defend you. Now tell me why you followed me here."

"I felt guilty that I'd let you know I had a problem," the hermit told him. "And I came to see what happened to the three of you. I thought I might be of some help. Since you all seem in good shape, I'll see what shape my cave is in now."

He stepped into his cave. The donkey followed him.

21

The cave was just as the hermit had left it. "Perhaps the doorway was too small for the dragon," Brother Donald said. "Or he might have thought he'd choke on his own smoke in here. Anyway, I have bowls and spoons if you'd like to stay for lunch. You won't have to wash your ears afterward, Jay."

Jay laughed. "Thank you, but I'm still full of porridge."

"I'm not hungry either," Sir Miles said. "I haven't recovered from the excitement of meeting the dragon."

Serena wasn't hungry either. She was afraid she'd brush against the donkey by accident and turn him back into a fiery dragon. He seemed to be avoiding her too.

"Jay," she whispered. "I think he likes being a donkey!"

"Sh-sh!" Jay went over to the knight. "Why don't we hit the trail, Sir Miles? You may meet somebody who needs to be rescued."

"You don't need the armor now, Sir Miles, and neither does Rocky," Serena said. "Come outside and I'll help Jay get you out of that heavy outfit."

When the armor was once again packed away in the saddlebags, Sir Miles started to lead the horse down the steep path. Serena and Jay waved good-bye to Brother Donald and followed the knight to the lane at the foot of the cliff.

The lane was next to the winding stream. As they went along, it was joined by other streams and became wider and deeper. After an hour, the stream had become a shining lake.

Willow trees grew on the bank here.

The lane curved away from the water.

"It's so beautiful," Serena said. "Let's stop and rest for a little while."

Sir Miles tied the horse to a willow tree. Rocky bent his neck to drink the cool water of the lake.

Serena and Jay sat on the bank under the tree, took off their sneakers, and dangled their feet in the water. Sir Miles decided to copy them.

They wiggled their toes in the clear water. A school of minnows swam past.

"Too bad I didn't bring my drop line," Jay said. "There must be bigger fish here too."

Suddenly all three of them heard a splash. They looked up, expecting to see a fish leap out of the lake. Instead they saw a lady rowing a little flat-bottomed boat.

She was quite close to them. It was strange that they had not heard her coming.

Sir Miles stood up and bowed. Then he put on his shoes.

The lady waved. "You are strangers here," she said. "I am the Lady of the Lake. What can I do to help you?"

22

Serena and Jay hurried to put on their sneakers.

Sir Miles bowed again. "Thank you, My Lady. I do not need your help, but these two young people do. I did not know where to look for you."

The Lady smiled. "When the pure in heart seek me, they find me. I see you are a knight-errant, sir. I've already learned of your good deeds. If you want to continue your adventures, you may leave your friends with me. I will do my best to help them."

"I'm sorry, Serena and Jay," Sir Miles said, "to have to part from you."

"Thank you for bringing us here. We

would have been lost without you,"
Serena told the knight.

"You're very brave, Sir Miles," Jay said,
"but please be careful."

The knight mounted his horse, and the
children patted Rocky's nose. Serena was
startled when the horse gave her a solemn
wink.

Sir Miles rode down the lane to where
it curved away from the lake. Then he
turned and waved to them.

Jay and Serena waved back.

The Lady of the Lake waited until the knight was out of sight. Then she said, "Come with me in the boat. You can tell me your story as we row along."

Jay grabbed his sister's hand to keep her from stepping into the boat. "How did you learn about Sir Miles's good deeds, Your Ladyship?" he asked.

"From my friends, the birds," she told him. "They bring me tidings they think I should know." She laughed. "I loved the story of how you bested Morgan le Fay. She hates me, you know."

"Why?" Serena asked.

"She loves everything evil," the Lady explained. "She is half-sister to the King. Secretly she hates him, just because he is noble and good. She hates me because I have saved him as well as some others from her wicked enchantments. She is also annoyed because humble creatures are under my protection. When she turns someone into an animal, I make sure it's a friendly one."

Serena liked everything about the Lady of the Lake. She stepped into the boat and pulled Jay in after her. They sat down and picked up the oars.

Jay and Serena rowed with their backs to the front of the boat.

The Lady sat facing them and told them which way to steer. "The birds watched what happened with the apples," she said, "and they heard you talking to the knight, but they couldn't understand what you were talking about. Maybe you can tell me what your problem is."

23

When the little boat was far from the shore, Serena and Jay stopped rowing and let the boat drift while they told the Lady of the Lake about the enchanted book.

She was leaning back and resting on one elbow to listen. When Serena started to describe the beautiful cover of the book, the Lady sat up and leaned forward. She looked around to be sure there was no one near enough to hear. "Speak softly," she whispered. "Perhaps we should go into my palace. Even Morgan's poisonous water snakes won't be able to hear us there."

She put an oar into the water. "Row as fast as you can. I'll steer."

Jay and Serena started to row. The little boat went skimming across the lake. When they reached the middle, the Lady gave a twist to her oar that made the back of the boat rise and the front take a nose-dive into the water.

The children tried to stop rowing, but they only seemed to row faster and the boat went down and down into the lake.

The water was as clear as air, but when they looked up, they saw swirls of green water instead of the blue sky.

Ahead of them was what looked at first like an enormous white rock. When they came closer, they saw that it was a marble palace, with carved balconies and delicate towers.

The boat coasted to a stop before an arched doorway. The Lady of the Lake put down her oar and stepped out of the boat. "Welcome to my palace," she said. "Come inside and have something to eat. Here you can tell me your story without fear of being overheard by one of Morgan le Fay's evil followers."

Suddenly both children realized that they could hear the lady just as if they were not underwater. And they didn't seem to be wet either.

"Jay," Serena said. "This is the most magic place of all."

Jay just nodded his head and didn't answer her. He was trying to remember something Sir Miles had told them.

The two children followed the Lady of the Lake into a beautiful room. They sat on cushioned chairs of just the right size and ate delicious food from golden plates. The food was different from any they had ever tasted. And they could eat as much as they wanted without feeling even a little sick.

When the meal was over, they went into another room. This one was brightly lit by fires that weren't burning in a dish of oil or blazing from a stack of logs. And Jay was sure they weren't lit by electricity.

Serena didn't notice. She was too busy describing the beautiful binding of the magic book.

"Long ago my best friend was a queen who liked robes with green and lavender designs on them," the Lady in the Lake said. "But she never had one as beautiful as what you describe."

"Why aren't you best friends with her now?" Serena asked.

"No one has seen her for many years," the Lady said. "The wife of Oberon, Morgan le Fay's son, sits on my friend's throne."

24

"Tell us about your friend," Serena begged.

The Lady of the Lake smiled. "She wasn't as beautiful as Queen Morgan le Fay, but she was much more fun. She was always laughing and joking. And everybody loved her, except Morgan." The Lady was silent for a little while. Then she said, "Morgan hated her, just as she hates me. Once I stopped the King from putting on a jeweled cloak that Morgan le Fay sent him. It was enchanted and would have burned him to death."

"Just as that apple turned me into a dog when I bit into it," Jay said. "Enchanting people by giving them things seems to be her trademark."

Serena was thinking hard. "Jay, we have to go home, but I don't know how."

"Why don't you go back the way you came?" the Lady of the Lake asked.

"We were trying to work a spell and make a copy of a book," Serena told her, "but we did something wrong. Instead of copying the book, we walked into the picture on the cover of it."

"Then all you need is a picture of where you want to go," the Lady said. "I know someone who does wonderful little

100

paintings for books. You can tell him what your home is like."

Suddenly she stopped talking. For what seemed an age, she was quiet. At last she said, "I quite forgot. Time here in my palace is different for mortals from time in their own world. No one can say how long you have been here. You must stay with me. I know you'll be happy. Now I'm sure you are tired. I certainly am." She led them to a little room with two couches spread with soft featherbeds.

Jay and Serena took off their sneakers and lay down. The Lady of the Lake tip-toed out of the room.

But neither Jay nor Serena could fall asleep. They were still on edge from all the excitement of the day.

"You know something, Serena?" Jay said. "I remembered Sir Miles warning us to stay away from the palaces in the hollow hills, but I couldn't think what was supposed to be so dangerous."

"It was Sir Miles who left us with the Lady of the Lake," Serena reminded him.

"She didn't give him much choice," Jay said. "Don't go blaming Sir Miles. Anyway, I like the Lady. I wouldn't want to have missed knowing her for anything."

"Neither would I, Jay. At least we agree on that," Serena said.

In a few moments they were fast asleep.

25

When Serena and Jay woke up, they found a pitcher of warm water and a basin on a marble washstand in the room. Serena washed her hands and face and ran her damp fingers through her hair.

Jay looked at the water in the basin. "You left hairs in here," he said. "I should have washed first."

At once the dirty basin vanished, and a clean, dry one took its place. Jay poured water from the pitcher into it to wash.

Both children were hungry. They put on their sneakers and were about to go out of the room to get something to eat. Suddenly they noticed two chairs and a table set for two where the washstand had been a moment before.

Jay grinned. "I wonder what we'll get for breakfast."

The food didn't look like anything they'd ever seen before, but it tasted exactly like what they wanted when they put it into their mouths. Serena was eating waffles and honey, and Jay had blueberry pancakes with maple syrup. There were two silver mugs and a silver jug of milk on the table.

"I'm sure the milk would taste like anything we wanted it to," Jay said. "But what I want right now is just milk."

"Me too," his sister agreed.

The table and chairs disappeared as soon as they stood up.

"Let's explore," Serena said. They left their little room and walked through a number of rooms of all different sizes.

In the first room Jay and Serena saw a man seated at a tall desk. He was dipping a goose quill pen into black ink to letter words on the page of a book. At the start

of each paragraph, the man painted a big red and gold capital letter.

Another man in the room was painting pictures to go into the book. He used beautiful colors and real gold paint. The people, buildings, and landscapes were all small, but each tiny detail was perfect.

"I wonder if this is the man the Lady of the Lake was going to have paint a picture for us," Serena whispered.

Jay grinned. "Can you imagine Brooklyn painted like this?"

All the rooms were full of busy people working hard. There were men making armor. Others worked on swords with jeweled scabbards.

"The King's famous sword came from this workshop," one man proudly told the children.

In one room people were weaving tapestry. In another they were sewing beautiful clothes. A shoemaker bent over his bench to make a pair of shoes with long, pointed toes.

They watched a man putting loaves of bread into an enormous oven. The baker was covered with sweat from the heat.

"Why do you work so hard?" Serena asked. "I thought food here was magic, and you could even eat a waffle just by wanting to."

"What's a waffle?" the baker asked.

26

Serena tried hard, but she couldn't describe a waffle to the baker.

Jay said, "It's a kind of cake with little square dents in it. It's crunchy on the outside, and you eat it with honey."

"Is it fun to make?" the baker asked.

"Mom says it's as much fun to make as it is to eat," Jay told him.

"I bake because I want to," the baker said. "I like to knead the dough and watch it rise. Then I can punch it down again and twist it into different shapes. And I love the smell of bread baking. It makes me happy that a lot of people enjoy eating what I bake. They like to look at it as well as eat it."

"Do all the people here work just because they want to?" Serena asked.

"Why else would they work so hard? They're all interested in what they're doing, and everyone here is happy. If they had nothing to do, they'd be bored."

The baker smiled. "Of course, people your age like to play. Here you can do anything you want just by thinking about it." He picked up a loaf of bread and put it into the oven.

The next room was much bigger than any of the others. Jay and Serena saw people playing games, dancing, and even ice-skating. Their skates were made of bone and were tied to their shoes. The floor was marble in most places, but it became ice as soon as the skaters reached it.

"How about it, Jay?" Serena asked. "Are you in the mood for Rollerblades?"

A moment later the two of them were Rollerblading around the room.

Several of the ice skaters skated close to them to get a good view of what Serena and Jay had on their feet. After that they too were wearing Rollerblades. They seemed to find them even more fun than their bone skates.

"They didn't even know they wanted Rollerblades until they saw them," Serena said. "Jay, we'd better go home before we spoil everything for the people here."

Instantly the Rollerblades vanished.

"I know how you feel," her brother told her. "Sir Miles was right. This place is dangerous for us. We don't belong here."

Jay led the way back through all the rooms where the happy people worked. They passed the little bedroom where they had spent the night, and the beautiful rooms where they'd been with the Lady of the Lake. At last they came to the arched doorway and stepped through it into the waters of the lake.

Serena grabbed Jay's hand. "Horse and Hattock!" she cried.

"Horse and Hattock!" Jay said.

Hand in hand, they started to rise up through the green water. As they went, the water became darker and darker.

It was black when they reached the sur-
face of the lake and swam to the shore.

27

A low stone wall ran around the edge of the lake.

"This wasn't here before," Jay said.

"Don't you remember we're in a completely different time? The wall may have been built hundreds of years later. I wonder what time we're in now." Serena climbed out of the lake onto the wall.

She was about to shake herself like a puppy, but she found she wasn't wet.

Jay pulled himself up on the wall and sat there looking around. It was almost dark, but there were still a few pink streaks in the sky. Lamps started to come on here and there among the trees.

Beyond the trees on the other side of the lake, Jay saw a tall building with a water tower on top.

Both of them heard the wail of a siren and the honking of automobile horns.

"Jay," Serena said. "This is Prospect Park, and we're not supposed to be here after dark!"

Jay grabbed her hand. "Horse and Hattock?"

"Horse and Hattock!" Serena agreed.

Together they rose straight up until they were high enough to be out of the light from the street lamps.

114

They swam high over their neighborhood. When they were near their house, Jay said, "Tread air, Serena. We don't want to come down with a bang."

There was a little lean-to over the stairs from the kitchen to the basement of their house. The roof of the lean-to was below the back window of Serena's room. Serena remembered that she'd left the window open a crack so that Her Majesty could come back inside the house.

"Maybe if we speak softly we won't come down so fast," Serena said.

Jay thought about this. "We do always seem to be screaming the command."

"Hattock and Horse!" the two children whispered. They floated slowly down and landed softly on the roof below Serena's window.

Neither Jay nor Serena was tall enough to reach the windowsill.

Jay stood on tiptoe and whispered,

"Horse and Hattock!" Slowly he began to rise. When he was high enough to push up the window, Serena grabbed his legs to keep him from rising higher.

Jay opened the window. Serena let go of his legs.

Jay crawled into her room, whispering, "Hattock and Horse." He turned around and leaned out of the window to reach down and grab his sister's hands.

Serena walked like a fly up the outside wall of the house while Jay pulled her up to the window. Then she scrambled over the sill into her own room.

The magic book was lying open on the bed. Words appeared on the blank page.

I SEE YOU TWO HAVE
BECOME EXPERTS AT LEVITATION.
I COULDN'T HAVE DONE BETTER MYSELF!

28

Serena didn't answer. Instead she closed the book.

The moment she touched it, the beautiful binding dissolved under her fingers. Serena found she was holding on to a freckle-faced lady with thick red-gold braids, a turned-up nose, and a mischievous mouth. She was wearing only a sparkling crown, a white linen undergarment, and jeweled slippers.

Serena let go of the lady and tried to curtsy. This was difficult, because Serena was wearing jeans.

"What happened to my beautiful dress?" the lady asked in a voice that sounded like music.

"Your dress was one of Morgan le Fay's enchanted presents, Your Majesty," Jay told her. "It turned you into a book."

Her Majesty looked at the chalk circle on the floor with Mrs. Darby's mirror and the book of King Arthur still in the middle. She touched the chalk with her slipper. The circle vanished. "I guessed you two were meddling with magic. You'd better put those things away before your mother sees them. Then you can tell me what happened."

Serena put the mirror back on Mrs. Darby's dresser, dumped out Water, and found room for Earth in her desk drawer.

Jay let Air out of the latex glove. He stuffed the glove and Fire into his pocket and took the King Arthur book to his room.

Her Majesty sat on the desk chair and watched. When all signs of spell making were gone, she said, "Start at the beginning and tell me everything."

They took turns telling the story. When they had finished, Her Majesty said, "You

must have a very powerful charm to break those enchantments, Serena. I've never heard of anything but a four-leaf clover doing such a good job."

Serena had forgotten that she had put one into her pocket. She decided not to mention it now.

"I was right about that hill in Prospect Park," Her Majesty said. "It's hollow, and there's a lovely palace inside, but I can't go around like this in my shift."

Serena went to her closet and took out the fancy party dress. "This might fit you. Aunt Sally buys things too big for me so I can grow into them."

Her Majesty loved the fancy dress and thanked Serena. It was perfect for a queen, and she looked beautiful in it.

"Thank you again and good-bye. I have to make myself small until I reach the palace," Her Majesty said.

"Will we see you again?" Jay asked.

"We want to," Serena told her.

"Then you will," Her Majesty shrank to the size of a gnat and flew away.

"I wonder what her name is," Serena said.

"Try saying Rof backward and then Bam backward," Jay told her. "Then look up Bam backward in the dictionary."

Serena took the four-leaf clover out of her pocket. The paper cup was crumpled and dirty, but the little plant was still fresh and green. Next morning Serena planted it in the backyard.